THE
KINGDOM
NEW AND REVISED

DESTINY IMAGE® PUBLISHERS, INC.
P.O. Box 310, Shippensburg, PA 17257-0310

"Promoting Inspired Lives."

This book and all other Destiny Image and Destiny Image Fiction books are available at Christian bookstores and distributors worldwide.

For more information on foreign distributors, call 717-532-3040.

Reach us on the Internet: www.destinyimage.com.

ISBN 13: 978-0-7684-8108-2

For Worldwide Distribution, Printed in the U.S.A.

1 2 3 4 5 6 7 8 / 28 27 26 25 24

THE
KINGDOM
NEW AND REVISED

YOUR IDENTITY AND
INHERITANCE IN JESUS

WRITTEN BY JERRIANN WEBB,
ILLUSTRATIONS BY IRELAND R. CILIO

Glossary of super important words:

Identity: The first thing God gave us! We are made in God's image to resemble and represent Him. We are made in God's likeness to function and operate like Him. Read Genesis 1:26-28.

Inheritance: Gifts, promises, resources, and access to whatever you need from the King! Jesus died on the cross to forgive us of sin. How amazing! He also died and was resurrected so we could live a free and powerful life now! He has given us so many gifts, like the Holy Spirit! God wants you to know He has promises for you! He wants you to know what resources are available to you now as the King's kid!

Assignment: God told us who we are, and then He gave us something to do! We can all live like Jesus! We can showcase God's goodness in all we do and say!

Deception: Believing a lie and not even knowing it is a lie.

Catastrophic: A word used to describe something horrible. When sin entered the Kingdom, it caused a disastrous separation between God and His kids.

Domain: Your home!

The Last Adam: Jesus is the last Adam. Jesus came to restore the relationship Adam lost in the Garden. Jesus came and restored the Kingdom! See 1 Corinthians 15:45.

Dominion: Authority

Commission: God has authorized us as His sons and daughters to display His glory!

Shalom: Wholeness. Because of Jesus, we can be whole and happy.

Exponentially: Always increasing! God has new and wonderful gifts to give you every morning!

"I have a story to tell you, little ones," the daddy whispered.

"The bravest and loveliest of all stories!

A true story so you will know the true you."

There once was a Kingdom and it began with a King...

A magnificent, imaginative, wondrous King!

A King who is love, and who never could lie.

A King who is good. A King who is wise.

A brilliant Love King, full of delight!

Full of laughter and giggles and rapturous Light!

And the King spoke into darkness, "Let there be Light!"

He spoke and divided the day from the night.

And glorious King Creator then spoke into time

Joyously creating a garden of incomparable design.

Jaw-dropping splendor and exquisite displays

Of a loving Creator unsurpassed in His ways.

Patterns and hues, the greenest of greens!

Breathtaking landscapes, unparalleled scenes.

The King spoke such resplendence as the grasses, they grew!

They sang of His radiance! Trees with seed-bearing fruit!

And He looked at the oaks
and dolphins and sun.

He looked with great pleasure
at all He had done.

Dinosaurs and redwoods
stretching to the sky!

Waterfalls cascading and
bright butterflies!

And in the Garden, a people, a most precious creation.

The Creator now Father birthing a nation.

He made them like Him! Adam then Eve.

He put breath in their lungs and said, "You're like me!"

The King placed them in charge. There they belonged.

Destined to rule the Garden, their home.

And so, in the people, an assignment bestowed

From a Father so faithful from whom all goodness flowed.

Completion. Perfection. The Father's design.

The language of Heaven to be yours! To be mine!

And perhaps you know the story, you may know it too well,

Of a serpent accuser with deception to sell.

Thoughts creeping and seeping into Eve's mind.

You can be like God... who you are is a lie...

And with a turn of events, catastrophic infection
Entered the Kingdom through rebellious rejection.
In a deceptive and tempting, tantalizing bad trick
The deceiver deceived and made the world sick.

And Adam and Eve with regret and sad shame

Lost the key to the Kingdom and gave their domain

To a serpent, now foe, pride twisted, unfurled,

As the weight of the sadness ripped through the world.

And then heartache ensued, unimaginable pain

Seen in every generation and in each family name.

Oh, but the King! The King of pursuit!

He would never stop loving and looking for you!

He would go to great lengths to restore what was lost.

He would search for His beloved at passionate cost!

In the greatest love story to right what was wrong,

The King pursued His sons and daughters to bring them back home.

And Light broke through silence as King Father sent Son!

To redeem what was lost, to undo what was done.

In a move unsurpassed the Last Adam He came!

A Man had to get back what a man gave away.

And there in the manger
a Savior's heartbeat!

And there on the cross
our freedom complete!

And out of the tomb
dominion then won!

A commission to reign
as daughters and sons!

The King resurrected a Kingdom in you and in me!

Jesus now Lord of a people redeemed!

Rest and shalom. Connection again.

Our identity found only in Him.

A new Kingdom nature! Royal and true!

Holy Spirit given to empower you!

Immeasurable inheritance, a gift from the King!

Within you God's Spirit can live and can sing!

And now...

There is a Kingdom. It is fully restored,

And you are the heir of exponentially more

Than you could ever imagine cause the Kingdom is near!

We can all live like Jesus cause the Kingdom is here!

And the King calls you friend! You are lovely and kind!

You are righteous in Christ! And you have the King's mind!

You are a solution to a world who needs you.

You carry His power. You know what to do!

You have authority. You now have the key.

Son and daughter, today, see what He sees!

Let your light shine

Speak and speak up as your future unfolds!

Be brave and courageous! There are feats to be told

Of all the King will do through you, through your life!

He has positioned you now at this moment in time...

...to know who you are in the Kingdom.

The world is waiting for you.

Discussion Questions

God has a wonderfully wild plan for your life! What are some things you think He is calling you to do?

When do you feel the love of God the most? When you're outside? Praying with your family? When you're at church? When you're laughing?

FOR GIRLS: God was not confused when He made you a girl! God has made you a girl for a specific purpose! Name all the ways you love being a girl!

FOR BOYS: God was not confused when He made you a boy! God has made you a boy for a specific purpose! Name all the ways you love being a boy!

Jesus has rescued you from the kingdom of darkness so you can live in the Kingdom of Light. How can you remember this truth every day?